BITTER HONEY

Helen Brooks

Harlequin Books

TORONTO • NEW YORK • LONDON
AMSTERDAM • PARIS • SYDNEY • HAMBURG
STOCKHOLM • ATHENS • TOKYO • MILAN
MADRID • WARSAW • BUDAPEST • AUCKLAND

Special thanks and acknowledgment to Helen Brooks

ISBN 0-373-15301-5

BITTER HONEY

First North American Edition 1995.

This edition Copyright © 1995 by Harlequin Enterprises B.V.

Copyright © 1993 by Helen Brooks.

This edition published by arrangement with Harlequin Enterprises B.V.

® and TM are trademarks of the publisher. Trademarks indicated with ® are registered in the United States Patent and Trademark Office, the Canadian Trade Marks Office and in other countries.

Printed in U.S.A.

One

"Paige? Your stepfather's party... There was something I forgot to tell you..." As her mother's soft warm voice faltered on the line, Paige felt her antennae buzz. "It's Declan."

"Declan? What's he got to do with Gerald's fiftieth birthday party? I thought he'd forgotten where you both lived! You mean he might actually honour us with his presence? America's loss is our gain and all that?"

"Paige..." The deep sigh caused her a moment's guilt. But they *were* talking about Declan Stone! "Please, darling. Declan is Gerald's son, after all. It's only natural he should be here."

"I couldn't agree more," Paige said tightly. "It is also natural that he should visit you both occasionally. He flies between America and England at least once a month to my knowledge."

"Darling, please don't upset yourself. Accept Declan for what he is. I have." Brenda Stone thought Paige had just taken a childish dislike to Declan that had grown with the years. That was fine and exactly the way Paige wanted it. "Goodbye, then, dear. We'll see you tomorrow." Paige caught the soft sigh as her mother replaced the receiver.

Blow you, Declan! she thought. Why did you have to turn up like the proverbial bad penny?

She could never hear his name without thinking of that first time she had seen Gerald's son. She had been sixteen, painfully shy, her face covered in freckles and the odd adolescent spot, huge horn-rimmed glasses hiding her eyes, her hair pulled back in a ponytail and a brace on her front teeth.

He had been a devastatingly adult twenty-four, cool, charming and with something dark and mysterious in his make-up that appealed to a romantic sixteen-year-old.

It had been her first visit to Gerald's beautiful country house in rural Hertfordshire since he had started courting her mother two months before, and she had been overwhelmed by the opulent lifestyle. So had her mother. The two of them had crept through the vast, exquisitely furnished rooms with something akin to awe.

Gerald had thrown a pool party in his massive grounds and a barbecue for some of his friends to meet her mother, but Paige had developed a headache and returned to the house, half hoping, she admitted secretly to herself, that she might see Declan alone before he returned to London. It was her first experience of a "crush" and she was finding it painful.

"I don't understand you, Father!" She heard Declan's voice first. "What the hell are you thinking of?"

They must be in Gerald's study, she thought quickly as she stood hesitating in the wood-panelled hall. She was turning to leave when Gerald said, "I love Brenda, Declan. What's wrong with that?"

"Nothing." She heard a chair being scraped back abruptly. "You're still a young man, Father. But marriage? You've only known the lady eight weeks! What makes her so different from all the other gold-diggers who have been after you since Mother died?"

"That's enough, Declan." Gerald's voice was tight with irritation. "Brenda's a wonderful woman. The others *were* different. There wasn't one I could envisage spending the rest of my life with. Until now.''

"Well, isn't that just dandy?" The voice sounded closer, but for the life of her Paige couldn't move. "You don't think it's wishful thinking, do you? I don't trust that dewy-eyed helpless angle the lady does so well. I've got a nasty idea it's hiding the pound signs in her eyes. I don't like her and I don't trust her, and as for that awful daughter!" There was a harsh bark of a laugh. "Do you seriously expect me to acknowledge *that* as my stepsister?''

"I'm not listening to any more of this," Gerald said furiously. "I'm going to ask Brenda to marry me and if you can't accept that, then I suggest you make yourself scarce, boy. I won't have her upset in any way.''

"I'll do just that!" Declan growled. "I don't much want to see the mess you're going to make of your life anyway.''

Paige had found her legs at that point, flying up the staircase to her room and locking the door behind her. He thought her mother was one of those grasping women who would marry purely to secure themselves a fat bank balance! Her mother! Her sweet, gentle mother! She pounded the bed with her fists, her eyes dry and burning, her pain too intense for tears. *How dared he*? There wasn't a trace of any of those characteristics in her mother's make-up. If anything she was too generous to friends when they were having a job to make ends meet themselves. The swine!

Her brain refused to dwell on the brutal comment about herself but later, when they arrived home after all the excitement of the wedding announcement, her mother flushed with happiness, she went to her room and lay in the dark with her heart breaking. "Do you seriously expect me to acknowledge *that* as my stepsister?" She couldn't bear it. She knew she was plain, under-sized for her age, but, surrounded by her mother's love and good friends, it hadn't mattered too much, or she had tried not to let it.

It was a long, dark night and she didn't close her eyes once during it, but by the time dawn broke, she had left her childhood behind forever, and reached several irrevocable decisions.

Firstly, she would not tell her mother anything of what she had overheard. She must keep it to herself.

Secondly, she would take her A levels and go on to college; try for that fashion course that was so sought after. She *would*.

Thirdly, she would ask her mother to buy her contact lenses for her birthday, get her hair cut in a more flattering style, and be diligent in applying the cream the doctor had given her for her skin.

And fourthly, she would get even with Declan if it was the last thing she ever did.

Paige came back to the present with a little start of annoyance. She couldn't afford to daydream today; she had to finish these sketches and get them to the office before she left for the country tomorrow.

She had gone on from strength to strength with the firm who had employed her when she had left college twelve months ago, but was wise enough to understand that she was still very much a junior designer.

As the phone interrupted her again, she sighed.

"Paige? It's me, sorry. Were you working?"

"Of course, Matthew, what else would I be doing at half-past ten on a Thursday?"

"Yes, well, I just rang to say I might be a bit delayed tomorrow." Matthew's voice held that note of worried concern that was habitual with him. "Would your mother mind if we arrived eightish?"

"Not at all," Paige said shortly. "I'll let her know. Goodbye, then." She had put down the phone before he could reply—Matthew was apt to waffle on all day. A son of one of the partners in the firm she worked for, he was a hard worker and altogether one of the nicest people she had ever met. Blond good looks and a wealthy father hadn't spoilt him, and yet . . . She sighed to herself at the drawing-board. There was something missing, some . . . spark. She shook herself angrily. What was the matter with her today?

There was a bite to the evening air as Matthew's BMW drew up outside Gerald's house the next night. The long driveway was packed with cars but one stood out from the rest.

"Wow!" Matthew's eyes were fixed longingly on the sleek silver sports car as Paige glanced at him. "Who do you suppose owns that beauty?"

"Someone with more money than sense," Paige said practically. "The insurance alone must cost a fortune!"

As they walked arm in arm up the steps to the front door, she was suddenly immensely glad of his uncomplicated friendship. She smiled up gratefully into his face as the door swung open.

Paige glanced from the man at her side to the tall, dark figure in front of them and was conscious of the world standing still for a split-second, then roaring on at twice the normal speed, the noise of the party only faintly registering on her stunned senses.

"Good evening." Declan held out his hand and Paige took it mechanically. "I don't think we've met." She was thankful when he let go of her hand and shook Matthew's. "I'm Declan, Gerald's son, by the way."

"How do you do," Matthew answered for both of them; she was quite beyond speech, although her face portrayed none of the inner turmoil that was tightening her stomach into a giant knot.

"Come on, Matthew." She drew him towards the drawing-room, ignoring Declan, although aware of the stiffening of his big body at such blatant rudeness. The swift appraisal she had made told her he was subtly different from the brash young man she remembered. The square face was even harder than she recalled and there was a sprinkling of silver in the springy black hair that made the silver-grey eyes all the more startling. The aura that surrounded him was one of dark, controlled force.

"Paige?" Matthew looked troubled. "I don't understand. That was your stepbrother, wasn't it? Doesn't—?"

"Please, Matthew." She saw her mother approaching. "I'll explain it all later."

"Paige, darling..." Her mother hugged her close for a second before examining her more closely. "You look absolutely gorgeous, doesn't she, Declan?" She had known he would move to their side when he heard her name.

"Paige?" The moment was sweet and she savoured it. "*You're* little Paige?" The silver eyes were narrowed in wonder as they swept over the slender, full-breasted figure, smooth-skinned and long-legged with a mass of warm chestnut-red hair framing a heart-shaped face with huge hazel eyes. She had designed her dress and jacket herself and knew the rich cream silk suited her skin and hair to perfection.

The hated brace had assured a twenty-four-carat smile that she now switched on as she steeled herself to hold his eyes. "Of course I'm Paige," she said coolly. "What did you expect? A brace and ponytail? I left those *awful* things behind some years ago."

There was no trace of understanding in the piercing eyes. He clearly didn't remember his words of so long ago, and why should he? Paige thought bitterly. That careless cruelty was just part and parcel of this man. But she remembered. And he would pay.

"I wouldn't have recognised you—I *didn't*!" the deep voice said wryly. "I think I've been very remiss in not renewing our acquaintance before now." He smiled briefly at Matthew, who was watching the proceedings with unconcealed interest. "We haven't met for years," he explained.

"Remiss? I don't think so," she said coldly. "We aren't related, after all, and I'm sure we have nothing in common." She turned away and took her mother's arm as she slipped her hand in Matthew's, shutting Declan out of the charmed circle. "Where's Gerald?" she asked flatly.

"Paige! That was very rude," her mother whispered.

"Leave it, Mum, please." Paige softened her words with a little smile. "I promise to be a good girl now that's over, OK? He had it coming after all, ignoring us all for years and then acting like my long-lost brother."

"I don't think brotherly emotion prompted that interest," Matthew said drily.

The evening rolled smoothly on, with a buffet, then dancing to the little band ensconced in the large bay of the vast sun-room.

Paige caught sight of Declan's dark figure once or twice but turned away immediately, annoyed at the fluttering in her stomach that his presence induced. He approached her once for a dance, with a polite nod at Matthew, his smile fading as she stiffly refused.

"Paige, what *is* the matter with you?" Matthew asked. "I've never seen you like this before."

"I know, Matthew," she replied, sighing as her pulse-rate returned to normal. "We just don't get on, that's all. Please . . ." She knew she was behaving badly but there was something about Declan, a dark, controlled maleness, that set her nerves on edge. How could she explain that to Matthew?

She glanced across the room now and was suddenly transfixed by the silver-grey gaze. He was standing by the far wall, wine glass in hand and big body relaxed, his face unsmiling. For a second she held his gaze, her wide hazel eyes revealing her opinion of him far more adequately than words, and then she wrenched her glance away with a feeling of panic. Within seconds her view had been obstructed by gaily dancing couples.

"Are you all right?" Matthew said at her shoulder. "You're as white as a sheet."

He touched her gently on the arm as his other hand turned her chin so he could look into her eyes. "I thought we were friends? Paige, I know there's something wrong. Can't you share it with me?"

"If I could talk to anyone it would be you, Matt," she said quietly as the sudden rush of tears into the back of her eyes made her hands clench. What was the matter with her? She was acting like a child. "Maybe some day, yes?" She smiled into his troubled face. "I'd love a coffee."

"Won't be a tick." As he went through to the dining-room, she leant back in her seat with a small sigh. The warm, heavy air impregnated with expensive perfume and cigar smoke competed with the scent of hothouse flowers and suddenly it was too much. Without thinking she rose and crossed the room, making for the open glass doors that overlooked the garden. There was a long wooden bench just to one side and she sank on to it gratefully, lifting her face to the cool breeze. Matthew would find her here; she hadn't gone far. She shut her eyes for a moment.

"Alone at last." The deep sardonic voice right in her ear brought her eyes wide open as Declan sat beside her, stretching out his long legs and resting a casual arm along the back of the bench behind her. Nerves she had not known she possessed leapt into life at his closeness.

"What do you want?" she asked faintly.

"I want to talk to you. Is that permissible?"

"No! Yes, I mean . . . I'm waiting for Matthew," she said weakly. "He's bringing me coffee, so I can't—" Her voice stopped abruptly as he touched the heavy fall of red silky hair resting on her shoulders.

"Beautiful, quite beautiful," he said softly, his eyes wickedly sensual as they came to rest on her mouth.

"I'm glad you approve," she said as she stood up, her eyes as cold as ice. "Now, if you'll excuse me . . ."

"Not before you've answered something that's been bothering me all night," he said softly as he reached out and jerked her back down beside him. She glared at him angrily. *How dared he?*

"Do you mind?" she said furiously.

"I don't but you do, and that's what I want to ask you about." He shifted slightly and as he did, she became aware of the leashed strength in the big body so close to hers. The dark, rugged face was faintly piratical. Not handsome in a conventional sense, but there was a magnetism in the harsh, proud face that was powerfully seductive. She had never been in the presence of such charisma before and she didn't like it at all.

"Well?" She raised her chin as their eyes meet. "What is it?"

"To my knowledge we have only met three times, maybe four, in our entire lives," he said softly. "I don't remember exchanging more than a dozen words with you, and yet..." he stared at her keenly "... you clearly dislike me, have displayed extreme rudeness from the first moment we met tonight, and I want to know why. It doesn't add up."

"And everything adds up in your world? Always?"

"Maybe not, but don't change the subject," he said. "I can't believe you are a hard, cold woman. Those warm, full lips and that wonderful hair speak of passion, fire... Am I wrong?"

"Quite wrong." She eyed him furiously. "And why should I bother to acknowledge our tenuous relationship? Your father married my mother when I was sixteen and you were already an adult. We don't know each other, and you haven't bothered with your father or the rest of the family for years. I don't know you from Adam!''

"That could be easily rectified," he said mockingly. "I think I would like to get to know my little stepsister."

"Well, your 'little stepsister' doesn't want to get to know *you*," she said sharply. "And you are quite right, I do dislike you!"

The abruptness with which he moved caught her by surprise, and as she felt his firm, hard lips stroke her mouth fleetingly she caught a whiff of his lemony, sharp aftershave, then he stood up, his mouth smiling but his eyes as cold as ice. "Now that's a shame, Paige. But perhaps you'll change your mind."

"If that's what you're hoping for, you—"

"I'm not in the habit of 'hoping' for anything," he broke in smoothly. "When I want something I make sure I get it." She wasn't aware of her hand moving to her lips where the touch of his mouth was burning like fire, but as his eyes followed the action it registered and she brought her hand down, lowering her eyes. The man was a monster! He laughed softly, the sound somehow harsh. "But maybe I don't want you, Paige. You'll just have to 'hope' for the best, won't you?"

The mockery was too much and she reared up. "You don't impress me with your clever little speeches and veiled threats, Declan. Your type are ten a penny and just as cheap. Goodbye, Declan."

This time she took him by surprise, swinging on her heel with a lightning movement and striding off through the open doors into the bright lights. As she saw Matthew in the distance with a cup of coffee in each hand, she felt a rush of affection for the tall, very English figure that made her reach up and kiss his cheek as she arrived at his side.

"OK, sweetheart?" He smiled down at her slowly. "Drink that and then I'll have to be going. You're back on Monday, aren't you?"

"Yes." She nodded. "I thought I'd stay the weekend with Mum, but..." Her voice dwindled away. "I might come back early."

It was as she raised the cup to her lips that she saw Declan watching a few feet away, his face sardonic. It was obvious he had heard their conversation.

She *would* stay the weekend now. She didn't know if he would be around but it would make no difference.

As she waved Matthew off from the top of the steps Paige sensed, rather than heard, the body behind her and tensed. It *had* to be Declan.

"Isn't lover-boy staying the night?" the hated voice drawled.

She swung round in an instant with her hand raised, but he had anticipated her reaction and caught her arm easily. "Now, now..." he said. "Is that the way to treat your elders?" His eyes laughed at her angry face.

"Let go of me," she snapped.

"Are you going to behave yourself if I do?" he asked. "It wouldn't do for Brenda or Father to have their evening ruined because their children were fighting, would it?" The silver eyes roamed over her hot flesh. "Have you considered that in this ridiculous vendetta you seem to have against me?"

"I can be civil in front of them if I have to," she said tightly.

"And if I don't play ball?" he asked. "You may live your life on such a level but I don't like insincerity."

"Not even if it protects people you love?" she asked as he let her arm drop.

"Not even then." As she looked up at him she was aware of thinking that he wasn't as tall as she had thought. Five feet eleven, six feet maybe, but he gave the impression of being much taller. "If you expect me to go along with this little charade then I shall expect politeness at all times, Paige. Do you understand me?" There was no mockery in his face now. "I do not play games, I am too old for such trivia. You toe the line with me or take the consequences." He eyed her coldly.

She would have loved to snap back with a sharp comment but much as it infuriated her, he was holding all the aces. She *didn't* want her mother and Gerald upset and he knew it. How she hated him!

"How long are you staying?" she prevaricated.

"Do I take that as agreement?" he asked softly. "You intrigue me, Miss Paige Stone," he began lightly.

"My name is Paige *Green*," she said sharply. "I kept my father's name, although that is no reflection on Gerald. I like him very much, but he married Mum, not me."

"And exactly what does that mean?" Declan asked.

"It means that you are your father's son as I am my mother's daughter," she said softly. "Your father is enormously wealthy, and we had next to nothing, as I'm sure you're aware." The implacable face stiffened slightly. "I'm very grateful for all Gerald's kindness, but now I'm independent, and if anything should happen to either of them I don't want a penny of your father's money."

"Are you serious?" he asked grimly.

"Of course. Gerald wouldn't accept it at first, but I reiterated my feelings when I was twenty-one and he promised they would be respected. I don't need your family's money, Declan, and I don't want it."

"You must have hurt him," he said.

She stared at him in surprise. It wasn't the reaction she had expected. "I think it did at first, but I made him understand that it didn't affect what I felt for him as a person," she said slowly. "I like—no, love your father, Declan. He's as different from you as chalk from cheese."

"I can buy that," he said. "Why do you feel so strongly about all this, Paige?

"That's my own business," she said stonily.

"You're quite a mystery girl, Paige *Green*." His eyes narrowed on the lovely face in front of him. "And I don't indulge in social flattery. When I said you were beautiful I meant it. Can you accept that?"

"It doesn't matter one way or the other, does it?" She forced her voice to be cool although she was trembling. It was his closeness.

"Are you frightened of me?" he asked abruptly.

"Of course not," she said, but as he took a step nearer she backed away.

"You are, aren't you?" he muttered, eyes raking over her white face. "Who has been feeding you stories about me?" He was by her side now. "What have you heard?"

You'd be amazed at what I heard, she thought. But, "What is there to hear?" she said tightly.

"Oh, the usual things . . ." She had known he was going to kiss her again but had been powerless to stop it happening, and now as his mouth closed on hers she found herself drawn into his arms and held tightly against the hard body as his lips plundered hers. He certainly knew how to kiss, she thought faintly, and she couldn't, *mustn't* respond. She ought to be struggling, but instead, she found herself kissing him back.

There was a mastery, a deep sensual warmth in his lovemaking, and she felt herself responding to this thing she had felt from the first moment she had seen him at sixteen, before the hurt had burnt it away.

Suddenly the kiss was subtly different from anything she had ever known, and as his hands moulded her curves against his hardness in sensual familiarity, cold reason returned in an icy deluge.

"Stop, please stop..." She jerked herself out of his hold with a violence that almost made her fall, and as she opened the front door and stumbled through he was still standing on the second step, his face taut and his eyes bleak, his hands thrust deep into his pockets.

Two

She woke very early the next morning after just a few hours' sleep, but by the time she went down to breakfast she was, outwardly at least, the epitome of the cool, calm Englishwoman at home in the country. Her hair was secured in a shining ponytail, her figure encased in heavy cream linen trousers and matching shirt, her feet shod in smart brogues.

"Morning." Gerald was alone in the large breakfast-room. How did you sleep?"

"Fine, thanks." She smiled. "All alone?"

"Your mother never rises before ten, as you know," he said with a little frown of disapproval. Gerald had never been able to understand her mother's weakness for late mornings, but indulged her, with just the odd reproving remark now and again. They were still so much in love, Paige thought enviously, helping herself to scrambled eggs and bacon from covered dishes on the trolley beside the table.

"I was surprised to see Declan home," she said carefully after they had eaten in silence for some minutes. "Have things improved between you two?"

Gerald nodded. "I've your mother to thank for it all really," he said. "She contacted Declan and asked him to meet her in London a few days ago. I don't know what was said, but he came extending the olive-branch, which I was only too pleased to accept. I've missed him, Paige. Does that sound weak?"

"It sounds perfectly normal to me," Paige said.

"I have to confess I've never understood him," he told her. "His mother did, and they were very close. Still, that's often the way. Sons and mothers, fathers and daughters."

"Yes." But how could Declan have shut him out for years? It was heartless.

Her pulse leapt violently as the door opened and the object of her wrath entered.

"Father. Paige." Declan nodded to them both.

"I hope you slept well?" She nodded a reply and quickly averted her gaze. She just knew he was mocking her again. He knew how he had affected her last night.

"Paige?" She came to, to find Gerald smiling at her. "I asked you if you'd got any plans for today?" he repeated.

"Sorry." She returned the smile as her cheeks turned pink. "I was daydreaming. I thought I'd go into town and browse the shops, maybe go for a drive in the country if I can borrow one of the cars?"

"No need." Declan's deep voice broke in. "I'll take you."

"No!" The word shot out and she saw Gerald stiffen. Careful, Paige. "No, you don't have to do that," she hedged. "I haven't met a man yet who likes shopping, and I tend to dither—"

"I said I'll take you." He raised his eyes from his plate as he spoke. "It's settled."

"Oh." She heard the murmur with a dose of self-disgust. She had been out-manoeuvred by an expert and could only accept for Gerald's benefit. "Well, that's really kind of you, Declan," she said prettily. "I do hope you won't be too bored." Two can play at this game, she thought. "It will be so nice to get to know each other after all this time, won't it?" She saw Gerald relax.

"My thoughts exactly." There was a wicked innuendo in those words that was for her ears alone.

As she slid into the silver sports car Matthew had admired Paige had the strangest feeling she was sitting on a level with the road, and as Declan joined her in the driver's seat she was aware of hard-muscled thighs close to hers, the sheer male bulk of him uncomfortably close. What was it with him? she thought painfully. She had never had her femininity exposed so rawly before.

"Paige?" He had leant back in his seat and closed his eyes, and it was like this that he addressed her. "Do something for me, would you?"

"What?" she asked warily.

"Relax. You look scared to death and it makes me feel you expect me to leap on you at any moment. Now, while the idea is not unappealing, at 10:00 a.m. after a hearty breakfast, positioned in a car unsuitable for such activities, *and* right outside our parents' bedroom window, I think you can assume that you are pretty safe."

"You're a pig," she said weakly.

"You say such sweet things." He opened his eyes and turned to face her. "You look remarkably like a delicious little honey-pot," he said.

"All tasty and soft and silky, but I bet that if I tried a spoonful it would be bitter. For me at any rate. Am I right?"

She shrugged tightly. "You'll never know."

"And Matthew? Is he the current boy-friend?"

She shrugged again. "What is this? Twenty questions?" She turned to undo her window but searched helplessly until he turned the ignition key and flicked a switch to it automatically. "Thank you." She turned away, her face scarlet.

"My pleasure." He gave her one last look and then fastened his seat belt, easing the powerful car in a tight circle on the wide drive and then cruising past the avenue of trees to the open gates and the quiet country road.

"What direction shall I take? Town or country?" He glanced at her, silent by his side. "There are crossroads up ahead."

"Oh, I don't mind."

He gave an exasperated sigh. "Paige, this little trip was your idea, remember? Shopping and a drive in the country? Now which comes first?" But she hesitated, as they approached, and passed, the crossroads. "Decision made," he said calmly. "A drive in the country, lunch at a little pub I know and then shopping later. OK?"

"Look, Declan—"

"Do you like home-made steak and kidney pudding?" he asked cheerfully. "They do the best one I've ever tasted at the Horse and Penny, and the raspberry pie is out of this world." He eyed her quizzically. "And do drag a smile up when we arrive. The landlord is a friend and he'll think I'm losing my touch if you walk in looking like that."

"Huh!" The exclamation spoke volumes.

The approach to the small village was down a steep hill and they drew to a halt outside an unusual-looking pub.

"Jon is originally from Switzerland," Declan explained. "He married a local girl and they had only been here a year when the old pub burnt down. He rebuilt on the land and decided to go for an alpine look to remind him of home. Fits in well, though, doesn't it?"

"Yes, it does," she agreed slowly. The steeply pitched roof, decorative barge boarding and tile-hung upper storey did adapt to the limestone scenery all around. The magnificent garden, rich with colour and the drone of bees, was pure England.

"Sit down." Declan indicated a table for two. "I'll let Jon know we're here. Draught cider OK?"

"Fine." She perched uneasily on the edge of her chair as Declan disappeared inside. What was she doing here?

"There." Declan set a glass of cider down in front of her. "Smile, Paige, Jon is coming out in a minute." The tone was wry and she glared at his broad back as his friend approached.

"I'm pleased to meet you, Paige." The tall blond man had a heavy accent, but his round face was warm and smiling and she liked him instantly.

She smiled up at him and held out her hand. "I'm pleased to meet you too, Jon, and I love your pub."

"This is true?" He shook her hand and then turned. "I like your Paige, Declan."

"Good." Declan gave a small cynical smile. "But she isn't mine, Jon, not this one."

"No?" Jon smiled at Paige. "This is a pity. He needs a good woman, Paige."

"A bad one is more fun," Declan drawled. "Just because you're an old married man, don't consign me to the same fate."

"I have some news for you," Jon said proudly. "I am soon to be a father too. In November."

In the ensuing congratulations and back-slapping Declan's remark was forgotten, but as they sat waiting for the meal she remembered his dry, cynical voice, and darted a quick glance at him.

"Well?" He stretched his legs and took a long pull of cider. "What was that look for?"

"That remark you made to Jon about not wanting to get married," she said carefully. "Were you joking?"

He stared at her for a long moment, then he shrugged. "I've got nothing against marriage for those who need it," he said slowly. "It's just not something I'd indulge in myself."

"Why not?" In for a penny, in for a pound, she thought wryly.

"I prefer to keep my options open and my life uncluttered," he said. "I answer to myself alone."

It was said with such coldness that she blinked. There was an icy aloofness about him now that intrigued her even as she told herself to forget it. He meant nothing to her, what did it matter anyway?

"Here's the meal." As Jon approached with a loaded tray Declan switched back to attentive companion. He was such a complex man, able to mask his emotions at will, totally in charge of himself and the world around him. She would ask her mother about him later. It wouldn't do any harm. And it might give her an edge.

He stood up suddenly and leant over the table, loosening her hair and slipping the ribbon in his pocket. "What...?" She raised a hand to her hair as it fell in silky waves about her face.

"I like it loose," he said softly, "and if I had asked you to wear it like that you would have refused." He smiled humorously at her angry face, the first real smile she had seen. It transformed the harsh features in a way she could not have imagined.

"You really are the most impossible man I've ever met."

"Do you know, you aren't the first to say that?" he said.

The raspberry pie was as delicious as he had said but eating was difficult. Her mind was filled with so many conflicting emotions it was making her head ache, and the physical sensations Declan induced were more worrying than pleasant.

"You don't smile much, do you?" She had been unaware that he was watching her.

"It depends who I'm with," she said coldly.

"Ow!" He shook his fingertips as though they had been burnt. "You've certainly got a tongue on you, Paige Green. And a temper to match that glorious hair."

He stood up. "Coffee?"

"Black, please."

He disappeared back into the pub, and Jon carried the coffee out a few minutes later. "Declan is talking to Tricia for a moment," he said. "She is finishing a special sauce and then she will come to meet you."

"Oh...right." Paige smiled. "This is a lovely part of the world, Jon."

"I agree." There was satisfaction in the quiet words. "I shall like to bring up my children here. We owe Declan more than words can say."

"Declan? I don't quite follow."

"But you are family? I thought he would have told you..." His voice died away in embarrassment. "I should not have spoken," he finished. "Please forget it."

"Please, Jon. To be honest I would like to understand Declan better. We haven't had any contact in the last few years. If you can tell me anything that might help..."

"Well..." He sat down beside her. "I do not know if this will help, but as far as I know it is no secret. However, as he has not told you, I would prefer that you do not—"

"I won't say a word," she promised.

"We had not been here long when the premises were destroyed," Jon said. "Then we found we were grossly under-insured. The previous owners had not increased their insurance for years and we just took their figure.

"Suddenly we found that even with a mortgage and cutting cost rebuilding could not be done, and certainly not with the ideas I had. I had known Declan for years and somehow through a mutual friend he got to hear about it.

"The next thing we know he is down here with his cheque-book." Jon shook his head. "He wanted to *give* us the money, but we could not accept that, Paige."

"No, I suppose not," Paige said as her mind tried to take in the fact that he was talking about Declan, the whiz-kid financier, hard as nails...

"So he insisted on an interest-free loan, to be repaid at some future time, a 'gentleman's' agreement. And so..." he waved his arms expansively. "...the dream became a reality. He is a good friend," he finished soberly. "The best."

She was saved from trying to reply by the reappearance of Declan with a beaming Tricia. As the four of them sat and made small talk she glanced at Declan out of the corner of her eye as he laughed softly at something Tricia had said. How many men were there under that skin?

By the time she was settled back in the car as they prepared to leave, her thoughts were in turmoil.

"I hear you've done very well for yourself." He slid into his seat by her side and turned to her. "Brenda is very proud of you." The silver eyes caught her gaze.

"Is she?" Paige smiled. "I've had to work hard but it's worth it. I love my job."

He nodded slowly. "Design, isn't it?" As the engine purred into life he backed slowly out of the car park. "I was surprised you'd gone into that area. I'd had you down for a nurse, or nanny, or—"

The harsh words he had spoken so long ago came flashing into her mind wiping away the softer image as though by magic.

"Drudge?" she said crisply.

"Drudge?" He sounded genuinely amazed. "Of course not. It was just that I pictured you with people somehow, helping, looking after them, I don't know." He shrugged. "Still I hadn't seen you for years. People change a lot in their teens."

"This one certainly did." In her effort to keep all hurt out of her voice it sounded harsh, and he didn't speak for almost a full minute. By then his face was its usual sardonic mask.

"I remember a gentle, shy girl who wouldn't say boo to a goose. I guess you could say you'd changed."

"Gentle, shy girls get trampled on," she said bitterly.

"Someone hurt you?" He glanced at her.

"It was a long time ago," she said tightly.

"Are you interested in history?" Declan asked when the silence was deafening.

"History? I suppose so, sometimes."

"It's just that the next village is particularly steeped in it if you're tempted. There's a fine old manor house and a working smithy in the main street. Does that appeal more than shopping? It's up to you."

"Yes, okay." She glanced at her watch. "That would be better, actually. I don't want to be late back. Matthew is ringing at six."

"Is he? Well, we mustn't keep Matthew waiting."

She was going to explain that Matthew was phoning her to tell her the results of her latest designs, but in view of his unjustified derision she said nothing.

The house was beautiful and she especially liked the Turkish room, inspired by the private apartments of seventeenth-century sultans in Istanbul. "This has given me an idea for my bedroom," Declan drawled blandly. "After seeing the look on your face I think it would be a winner with the ladies, yes?" He smiled slowly, and the insidious pull at her heartstrings jerked uncomfortably.

She shrugged. "You need help in the bedroom?"

He laughed softly. "Not exactly, but atmosphere helps."

"I don't think—" She turned to make a light remark but found herself staring into his face instead, and there was something dark and warm in the narrowed eyes.

"Paige..." He cupped her face in his hands, bending down to take her lips as he did so, and as she felt their touch her insides melted. Like before, it was as though a flame ignited that would consume them both, and as the kiss deepened she felt she was drowning. The sound of other visitors approaching broke the spell, and as Declan moved away his face was rueful. "Come on, let's visit the smithy," he said.

She wandered round the old rough-hewn smithy in a daze, hardly listening to the skilled blacksmith.

As they walked back down the quiet leafy lane he took her hand in his. She felt like a schoolgirl on a date with an experienced man of the world, and the feeling intensified as she realised he had drawn her into a little shady dell hidden from the road.

"Declan, we need to get back," she insisted.

"It's too hot to get back in the car for a while," he said easily. "We've plenty of time. Have a seat." He indicated the carpet of thick springy grass and flung himself down, stretching out with his eyes shut.

She stood for a moment, uncertain of what to do next, and then carefully seated herself a few feet away. It was amazingly quiet in the secluded

little copse, and as the minutes ticked by she began to relax a little. Declan hadn't spoken since
he had lain down; in fact he seemed to have
dozed off. She peered at him now. His arms were
strong and sinewy. He must be very fit, she
thought idly. Very athletic, very vigorous... He
was an uncomfortable man to be around, she
decided as her eyes hesitated on his slim thighs.
Too potently male to ignore, too lusty...

The thought brought her head snapping down
as though she had voiced it out loud. What was
the matter with her?

She felt hot and flustered as she raised her
head again, this time to look straight into his eyes
as he raised himself slightly, propping his head
on his hand. "I thought if I relaxed you'd do the
same, but you're as nervy as a kitten," he said
slowly. "Are you always like this? No wonder
you're so slim."

"Not always, no," she said tightly. "Look,
Declan, I think we ought to be getting back." She
looked down pointedly at his hand now on her
arm, but he ignored the action.

"Relax, Paige, take a few minutes out of life
to relax." His voice was deep and husky, and as
she looked into the silver gaze she felt mesmer-
ised, unable to resist as his hand drew her inex-

orably down beside him. As his lips gently touched her creamy throat in soft burning kisses she felt herself begin to tremble, and then his mouth was moving all over her face, her ears, her neck, until she was almost begging him to take her mouth.

"You are the most tantalisingly delicious ..." His voice was lost as he claimed her mouth at last, moving over her so she could feel every inch of his body, his arousal obvious. She put her arms round his neck, drawing him even closer against her softness, and heard him groan deep in his throat as his body stirred against hers. His kisses were thrilling and she was barely conscious of his hands moving across her body, her whole being turned into one trembling whole of sensation. He broke away once to bury his face in the red silk of her hair but she searched for his mouth until his lips met hers, unaware of what she was doing, lost in this, her first taste of sensual pleasure.

"Hell, I must stop this, Paige." And the next instant he had sat up, running a hand through his hair, then springing to his feet. "That's enough. I'm sorry, Paige, I shouldn't have done that." As he stood looking down at her she saw a look of disgust on his face, and she was too inexperienced to recognise that it was directed at himself, not her. Her blood ran cold.

"Declan?" She too sat up, her cheeks burning. It should have been she who stopped the madness. He must think she was so easy.

Her thoughts were written on her face and he knelt swiftly at her side. "It was my fault. I should have known better. I've been playing with fire all day, but you're so damn sweet..." He stood up again. "Have you slept with anyone before, Paige? Matthew? Anyone?"

The question should have annoyed her but she only felt numb. Now their lovemaking had stopped she realised just how near Declan had come to taking her, and the thought was burningly painful.

"No," she said flatly.

"I thought not." The broad back was stiff as he still didn't turn his head. "Looking the way you do, in my world you'd be on your tenth affair by now."

"Would I?" Her voice was mechanical.

"I suppose I wanted to see if it was real," he said almost to himself. "You're so lovely, Paige, so unspoilt."

His words hammered on her mind. He had wanted to see if it was real! All this had been a game!

"I want to go home." She stood up slowly. "Now."

"Don't look like that." He reached across to touch her face, but she recoiled from him.

"Stay away from me, Declan." Her eyes blazed into his. "You've had your fun, you've proved that you could have taken me if you'd wanted to. Isn't that enough?"

"Paige. It's not like that—listen—"

"I'll *walk* home if you won't drive me!" Her voice was rising on the edge of hysteria.

"Okay, okay. We'll go now."

She sat huddled in the car all the way home, her face turned to the window. She had always despised the type of girl who fell into bed with a man on the first date, but now she realised that some of them, at least, might have been lost before a more experienced and clever mind. For *he* had known what he was doing.

And hadn't she? She almost groaned. Not really, no, she hadn't. She would never have believed that passion and desire were such strong weapons. Now she had been hurt twice by this man. She would make sure there was never a third time.

Three

December twenty-third. Paige grimaced to herself as she flung her portfolio on to an easy-chair. She hadn't been able to think of Christmas this year without her heart doing crazy somersaults at the thought that Declan might have the nerve to appear, despite the way they had parted company last summer.

Since August, she had been working non-stop anyway and it had proved a blessing after the disastrous weekend following Gerald's birthday. She hadn't had a minute to think or brood, but she had to admit that the constant hard grind was catching up with her. She'd have to slow down; Matthew had been saying it for weeks. Life was hectic and full but in spite of all that, there was something missing, and she didn't know what it was.

The churning feeling in her stomach was very much in evidence as she drove down to Hertfordshire the next day. It was bitterly cold but dry and sunny, and she drew into Gerald's drive just toward sunset. Declan's sleek car eyed her broodingly, the silver paintwork glowing pink in the reflection of the dying day.

He *was* here, then! Her nerves screamed in protest.

"You look peaky, Miss Paige." The housekeeper, Millicent's greeting didn't add to her confidence one iota and she pinched some colour into her pale cheeks before the door to the drawing-room opened.

"Paige, darling!" Her mother descended in a rush of softness and warmth and for a moment she had the crazy impulse to hide behind her skirts. "How are you? We hardly hear from you these days. You're working far too hard."

Paige emerged from her mother's hug with a bright smile and a little nod. "You're probably right, but I'm here for five days now so let's make the most of it. How are you and Gerald?"

"Fine, darling, fine." As Paige stepped into the room her head went up a notch and the smile became brittle. Declan was standing at the far end, one arm resting on the mantelpiece below which a roaring log fire crackled and spat, his dark presence dominating the colourful Christmas decorations and gaily festooned tree.

"Hello, Paige." The cool smile did nothing to warm the narrow-eyed stare that held her transfixed, and as he walked towards her she had to nerve herself to stand still. She held out her hand but he drew her carefully against him for a brief moment, kissing her cheek lightly. "You've lost weight."

"I've been working hard," she said tightly. "Deadlines to meet."

"Too hard." He frowned. "You'll make yourself ill." All this empty concern for her mother's benefit? she thought wryly.

"I'm a big girl now." With a cool smile she walked over to the fire. "Where's Gerald?"

"Delivering a box of goodies to little Mrs. Creedy in the village," her mother said quietly.

Once Gerald returned the evening passed without many awkward moments, but Paige declined her stepfather's suggestion of midnight Mass in the village. "I'll get to bed if you don't mind," she said quietly, eyes trained away from the dark, sardonic face opposite. She hadn't glanced at Declan once during dinner but had been aware of that silver gaze, which was sending goose-pimples down her spine. "Life has been hectic lately and I could do with catching up on some sleep."

"Fine, darling," her mother said quickly, and as Paige glanced up to smile her thanks she caught the worried glance that passed between Brenda and Gerald with a stab of guilt. This was going to be a wonderful Christmas, just wonderful, she thought bitterly, and it was all *his* fault! She looked at him now as she drained the last of her coffee and his silver eyes held hers tightly.

"You're leaving us so soon?" he asked smoothly. "Your mother has been on tenterhooks all day waiting for you to arrive."

"It's all right, Declan," Brenda said. "We've lots of time to catch up on the news and I'd rather Paige get some sleep for now. But it's sweet of you to be concerned." She touched his arm and Paige was amazed to see Declan smile back at her mother, the harsh face warm for an instant.

Sweet! She almost ground her teeth in her rage. He was about as sweet as a boa constrictor, and just as cunning.

She was still smouldering an hour later as she lay in bed, wide awake and furiously irritated.

Declan was dominating her thoughts to the point where she could have screamed with annoyance at herself. How she loathed him! She pictured the dark, austere face and hard, lean body and that strange little thrill shivered down her spine. "I *do* loathe him!" She sat up in bed and then groaned softly. Talking to herself again! She only did it round him. He'd send her mad if she weren't careful. And she needed some rest.

Christmas morning brought an exchange of presents that was embarrassing in itself. Paige had sailed down to breakfast after a troubled night, resolutely ignoring the headache lodged over her eyes and determined to act the perfect daughter. All went reasonably well until the unwrapping of the presents, although her first sight of Declan, cool and wickedly attractive in dark jeans and black silk shirt, was a nasty moment. It was as he handed her the tiny gold package enveloped in a gold bow that she felt a moment's panic. "You haven't bought me a present, have you?" she asked, her eyes wide with horror.

"Just a little trinket," he said smoothly. The "trinket" turned out to be a pair of beautiful antique ruby earrings that must have cost him a small fortune. Paige felt mortified. Why hadn't she thought to get him something? She had been so determined not to think of him that she had done too good a job! And now she felt awful.

"I haven't got you anything." She glanced up into his dark face. "I'm sorry, I've been so busy and I wasn't sure you'd be here."

"No problem." He smiled easily. "What can you buy for the man that has everything?" It was said lightly, but it was true! He was self-sufficient, satisfied with his life, master of his own destiny and yet, sometimes, when he let his guard slip, there was a vulnerability to the hard mouth, a yearning... She caught herself in amazement. Vulnerable—*Declan*? She really was beginning to crack up!

The lunch was delicious but Paige ate very little of it. There was a large lump lodged in her throat and her headache was worse. It was the worst Christmas she had ever had, when it should have been the best. Her career was taking off with a vengeance, and her mother and Gerald were the happiest she had seen them, thanks to the healing of the rift with Declan. But therein lay the root of all her problems. She caught his eye over the festive table and he raised a glass to her. "Merry Christmas, Paige."

"Thank you." She eyed him sourly. "The same to you."

"Many thanks." She could see that he was struggling to check his amusement, and then, as he continued staring at her, his expression changed. The silver eyes were suddenly softer, warmer... She blinked and lowered her eyes quickly. He was the original wolf!

"I'll help with the dishes." She marched out into the kitchen with her head held high. Millicent was spending Christmas with her sister in Devon. Paige leant against the sink for a moment, looking out into the stark, cold world outside which reflected exactly how she felt inside. Naked, vulnerable, frightened...

When she surfaced out of a deep but strangely uncomfortable sleep the next morning, the whole of her body was aching. Her head was throbbing, her legs felt like lead and she longed to stay in bed.

Gerald, her mother and Declan were already in the breakfast-room when she opened the door, but suddenly the smell of food was revolting to her.

"Don't you feel well?" her mother asked.

"Just a cold coming, I think." Paige tried a smile but the effort was too much. "I'll skip breakfast—just a cup of coffee, please." She couldn't be ill. Not now. Not in front of Declan.

"How about a piece of toast?" her mother asked. "It might settle your stomach."

"I don't mind." Paige looked at the empty toast rack. "I'll get some." Her voice was dull and heavy. Paige's legs suddenly seemed devoid of all feeling as she walked into the kitchen and placed two slices of bread in the toaster. When the door opened, she knew it was Declan.

"When are you going to stop this childish behaviour?"

"What?" In her surprise she looked straight at him.

"I said when are you going to stop this play-acting?" he bit out grimly. "I can accept I'm not your favourite person and in future I'll make damn sure I'm not around when you visit, but couldn't you just try to make your mother's Christmas a pleasant one? She's looked forward to having you home, although exactly why defeats me! As spoilt brats go you sure take some beating." He eyed her with searing disgust.

"Look, Declan—" He broke into her angry words as though she hadn't spoken and as she looked at him she was aware that she felt very ill. She would have to sit down . . .

"I suppose you're going to skulk off to your room to avoid being with me?" he continued tightly. "Well, what about... Paige?" As she began to fall she was conscious of the change in his voice but she was past caring. A deep roaring blackness was coming up to meet her and she had no energy to fight it. She couldn't have quite lost consciousness because she was aware of Declan catching her, and then his voice, calling for their respective parents. The rest was confused. Declan carrying her to her room, her mother undressing her, and then the arrival of a stern doctor who mellowed slightly after examining her in spite of its being Boxing Day.

"This nasty flu that's about," she heard him say in a loud whisper to her mother as he left the room. "Coupled with the fact that she's obviously quite exhausted." Her headache was blinding, her back was breaking and her mind was filled with cotton wool.

She slept all that day and the next in a daze of aching limbs, weird dreams and the endless drinks her mother presented at regular intervals, her relief at not having to face Declan paramount.

On the morning of the third day she awoke feeling a little more like herself. The grinding headache was gone, though her limbs felt as though she had been stamped on by a herd of horses.

"Paige?" Her mother's look of relief brought a feeling of guilt. What a Christmas! "Are you feeling better?"

"Heaps," Paige exaggerated quickly.

"Not well enough to go out, though," her mother said, plumping up her pillows.

"Go out?" She put a hand to her forehead. "The theatre? Declan's treat. I forgot." On Christmas Eve he had announced a Christmas present to them all of a trip down to London for theatre and a first-class hotel overnight. And tonight was the night. Or wasn't, in her case. "I'm sorry, Mum," she said honestly, "I just don't think I could make it."

"Of course not," her mother agreed briskly. "We can go some other time."

"Don't be silly." The thought of twenty-four hours by herself was actually quite attractive. "You must all go. I can see to myself for goodness' sake. I'm over the worst now."

Paige was surprised to find herself drifting back to sleep in spite of having done nothing else for nearly forty-eight hours, and when her mother came in later and whispered something in her ear she was aware of making what sounded like a sensible reply. It was mid-afternoon when she surfaced again and the house was quiet. They'd gone. She tried to remember what her mother had said. "Fridge stocked—" and something "—was at hand." She couldn't remember hearing the rest of that sentence.

She climbed out of bed carefully, remembering the weakness of the morning, and was annoyed to find it was still with her, along with a peculiar swimming sensation in her head. She felt sticky and hot and the thought of a bath was too good to resist. Her bedroom boasted a little *en suite* with a shower but the main bathroom on this floor had a sunken bath that was sheer luxury, and that was what she needed.

By the time the water was running into the bath her heart was pounding as though she had run a mile and a strange feeling of disorientation was making her light-headed.

The mirror tiles showed a small bedraggled figure with huge eyes staring back at her under a mass of tangled red hair. She'd wash her hair too. And then—

"What the hell do you think you're doing now?"

The shock of hearing Declan's voice right in her ear sent her toppling off the edge of the bath and into the foamy water, her nightdress and dressing-gown holding her down as she tried to surface. She was suddenly yanked, firmly and roughly, into a sitting position and opened dazed hazel eyes to see his furious face. "You're ill! You shouldn't be out of bed, let alone having a bath by yourself! Haven't you got a grain of sense?"

"Stop shouting at me." She tried to sound defiant but spoilt the effect by bursting into loud, uncontrolled sobs. Declan lifted her, dripping wet and shaking helplessly, into his arms, and sat holding her as he seated himself on the nearest thing, which happened to be the loo.

"Don't, Paige, don't cry," he said, reaching for a large bath-towel to wrap round her. "I'm sorry, I shouldn't have shouted but you scared me half to death sitting there like the ghost of Christmas past. I thought you were going to pass out again."

"I nearly did with you bellowing like that," she said. "I thought I was by myself. You shouldn't be here."

"Your mother told me you knew I was staying, that you'd agreed," he said quietly. "I insisted they went to the show. There was no need for us all to miss it and your mother needed a break.''

"Yes." Her hair was dripping water down her face, and she was aware that she had soaked him too. "I must have been dozing when she told me. I remember her coming in but that's all." She stared at him miserably.

"Paige?" His voice was husky. "The apologies are mounting up, aren't they? I'm sorry I didn't believe you were ill. I thought—"

"I know what you thought," she interrupted. "It doesn't matter..." She swayed slightly and steadied herself on the edge of the washbasin. "Can I have a bath now?"

"Don't be so ridiculous. You can barely stand up."

"I need a bath, Declan, and I must wash my hair now, it's wet anyway." She looked at him. "Please, I feel horrible." Her bottom lip trembled.

He sighed impatiently as he stood up, glancing down at his damp trousers. "Well, only if you agree to keep the door unlocked and allow me to stand sentry duty outside," he said. "My old robe is hanging behind the door. You can use that when you get out."

"I don't want—" But he had gone, shutting the door as he left.

She didn't linger in the warm silky water but felt altogether different when she opened the door ten minutes later swathed in Declan's towelling robe and with her hair wrapped turban-fashion. He was waiting, as promised, and the way the damp cloth moulded to the strong, powerful line of his legs and inner thighs suddenly made her feel quite hot.

"Now you dry your hair and get into bed while I bring you some toast," he said firmly as he walked her back to her bedroom.

"Declan!" She shook his arm off as they reached the door. "I'm not an invalid! I'm going to get dressed and come downstairs."

"I'm not arguing with you, Paige." He scowled. "I've been reasonable, now you do as I tell you. You've had a bad attack of flu made worse by being totally run-down in the first place. Now get in bed and stay there for the rest of the afternoon. You can get up this evening," he added, pushing her through the open doorway, "if I consider you're well enough."

"You can't tell me what to do!"

"Shut up, Paige." He cast one more furious look at her pale face, then turned and left, returning a few minutes later with a tray containing two slices of buttered toast and a glass of freshly squeezed orange juice. He deposited the tray on her lap without speaking and walked out again, his expression saturnine.

It was dark when she awoke and she was aware straight away that she felt much better. It was nearly seven o'clock. He must be downstairs.

She swung her feet out of bed and, although a faint weakness remained, there was no dizziness. She dressed quickly in jeans, blouse and knee-length cardigan, looping her hair into a high ponytail and not bothering with make-up, then walked downstairs on slippered feet.

The drawing-room was deserted, but the smell of cooking drew her to the kitchen, and as she opened the door Declan turned from the stove. "Paige? What the—?"

As she looked at him she had the strangest feeling that he was surrounded by an aura of light and then he was at her side, almost lifting her into a chair. "I told you to stay in bed!" She stared back at him silently as the dizziness receded.

"I feel much better," she protested weakly. "I was all right till I saw—"

"Me?" he finished. "Thank you *so* much. I do take it the feeling I inspired was not one of feminine weakness at my irresistible male charm?" He was joking at his own expense, but he was a little too near for comfort if only he had known it.

"Are you still that frightened of me?" he asked quietly. "There's no need to be. I wouldn't hurt you."

It was the ultimate in irony coming from him, and she lowered her head without replying.

"Would you care for a glass of wine?" His voice was cool.

"Thank you." She nodded and he poured a glass from the half-empty bottle on the table, refilling his own.

"Steak and salad suit?" He checked the two juicy steaks sizzling under a very low grill. "I thought it was time you ate, and of course I need to keep up my strength." He was being deliberately provocative and she ignored the innuendo.

"Steak and salad sounds lovely," she said and took a sip of wine.

"Good." He expertly tossed the prepared salad in a big wooden bowl, adding oil and seasoning.

"Do you like cooking?" she asked quietly.

He nodded. "Doesn't fit in with your mental picture of me? Well, it so happens I do. At home." He continued. "And I don't mean here. Home is a tenth-floor apartment in a high-rise in the middle of New York. Not everyone's cup of tea, but it suits me."

"What sort of food do you prefer?" she asked.

"Chinese. But it's difficult to get the flavour just right. One little slip and the flavour of a dish is ruined."

"Oh."

He didn't speak again as he busied himself with plates and crockery and it gave her time to warn herself to be careful. His charm was lethal, and never more so than when he was unaware of it, like now.

Four

"Was that my excellent cooking or were you just famished?" Declan smiled down at her empty plate.

"Both." Paige smiled back. "I'll load the dishwasher and clear up."

"No way." He pushed her back down in her seat.

"Coffee?" He indicated the machine. "You go through to the drawing-room—there's a fire—and I'll bring a tray."

When Declan entered a few minutes later she saw the black eyebrows raise fractionally as he glanced at the empty settee by the fire, but his face was expressionless as he settled the tray on a low coffee-table.

"Comfortable?" The meaning was unmistakable.

"Perfectly, thank you." She shifted slightly in the easy-chair.

"Come on, Paige," he said. "I've no doubt where I stand with you, but this is taking things too far. I've no intention of calling across the room to you. Come on."

She rose slowly and seated herself gingerly next to him.

"Do you get tired of men telling you how beautiful you are?" They had been sitting watching the flames as they sipped the coffee.

"Beautiful?" She turned slightly to face him. "Beauty is skin-deep, Declan. It's unimportant." There was no arrogance or false modesty in her tone, just a deep sincerity as she spoke the truth of the lesson she had learnt years ago.

"There are few people who can surprise me these days, Paige, but you are a constant revelation."

He had taken her mouth before she could reply and then there was only sensation as he drew her into his hard frame and she felt the shock of his arousal. His breath was warm and pure as he covered her face in tiny urgent kisses that lit a flame of wild excitement, and as his mouth returned to her half-open lips she heard herself moan with a feeling of helplessness. He felt so good, so warm, so alive.

"You're like a drug to me, Paige, so help me..." His breath was a shuddering sigh against her hot cheek and there was a slow-growing heat inside her that was destroying the ability to think, to question.

"Declan, please... I don't want this... What gives you the right to think you can treat me like...?"

"I thought I was treating you like a woman, Paige, a beautiful, desirable woman who wanted—"

"Wanted what?" she interrupted him. "You think you're irresistible, is that it? That I should be grateful to stand in line with all the others?"

"Now just a damn minute!" He rose abruptly. "I've never yet made love to one woman when I'm involved with another one and I sure as hell wouldn't start with you! Can you say the same?" The last words were aggressively hostile and she realised that he was talking about Matthew.

"I'm going to bed." She rose with immense hauteur which dissolved in a flash at his cruel laugh.

"Do I take it that is not meant as an invitation?"

He could joke, he could actually *joke* at such a time as this? "You're despicable."

"So? I really don't know what's the matter with you, Paige, but I'm getting tired of being made to feel like the original Marquis de Sade."

"The matter with *me*?" The injustice was too painful to ignore. "I suppose that day in the summer was a figment of my imagination, is that it? It never happened?"

"I wondered when we would get round to that," he said tightly. "I apologised—what more can I do?"

But she didn't want an apology, she wanted him to *care* that he'd hurt her. "Yes, you apologised," she agreed emptily.

"Paige? Can we talk about it?"

"There's no point," she said wearily. "I don't want to talk about anything with you, Declan."

"And that's the final line? No reprieve?"

"I don't trust you," she said. "I can't."

"The hell you can't! You *won't*—that's different."

"I'm not bandying words with you." The piercing gaze held her pinioned, although every instinct in her body was telling her to leave. There was something in the deep, rasping voice that was terrifying.

"Maybe talking won't get us anywhere," he agreed softly as he moved to stand in front of her. "You might despise and hate me, but we both know there's something between us that can render all your objections useless in the space of minutes."

"You mean sex?" she said baldly, trying to break the intimacy that had her longing to rest her head against that broad chest while his mouth covered hers. "Is this the line you give all your women?"

He swore, softly and succinctly, as he reached forward and took her in his arms and just for a second she was too surprised to react. One hand was tangled in the red silk of her hair, steadying her head for the penetrating invasion of his mouth, and the other was a rigid band round her waist. His lips were hard and fiery as they forced hers open for his tongue to explore the soft inner flesh of her mouth. His body cradled her close with a kind of fierce tenderness as though he needed to absorb her into his very being.

It was violent and consuming and yet tender, and she found herself racing in a hot, sensory intoxication that was as frightening as it was thrilling. Now his mouth was warm and sensual against her lips as his hands roamed where they would. Somehow her hands had found their place in the crisp darkness of his hair as she reached up to the broad, tense shoulders, and his hungry arousal became shockingly obvious as he pulled her into him so tightly that she could feel every inch of his muscled body against hers.

Paige knew it was up to her to put the brake on, but somehow she was helpless against his passion.

As they sank to the floor together she was conscious of one moment of sheer panic and then it was gone, lost in the feel and smell of him, the overwhelming need his body couldn't hide. His mouth was hot and insistent, but then the ache that his lovemaking had aroused was shattered as the harsh, shrill notes of the telephone exploded her back into the real world.

Declan froze and then moved off her in one swift motion that brought him upright as he snatched the phone and spoke into it in a sharp, clipped voice that was at odds with his shaking hands. As she sat up slowly he replaced the receiver and turned to lean against the wall with his back to her.

"Declan?" Her voice was a broken whisper.

"You see how it is?" he asked tonelessly. "You're playing with fire, Paige."

"Fire?" She glanced up at his broad back as she rose to her feet.

"Yes, fire," he snarled softly, turning to face her. "Keep away from me, Paige, do you understand?"

"But I thought—"

"You don't like me, Paige." He laughed humourlessly. "And who can blame you? We both know I'm no innocent but that's exactly what you are. The fact that I could seduce you is of no credit to me, and the fact that I want to, even less. Now just go."

"Go?" she repeated the word disbelievingly.

"Now!"

She heard the car start outside without believing it at first, but after sitting in stunned silence for a moment she leapt up and ran to the front door just in time to see a swirl of silver roar out of the drive. He had gone? He couldn't have. She turned abruptly and walked into the warmth of the house, shutting the door so violently that its bang vibrated the floor.

Later that night, after Gerald and her mother had arrived home happy and glowing, she escaped to her room. It was after midnight when she heard the phone ring and muted voices in the hall.

"Paige?" Her mother's light knock at her bedroom door caught her unawares. "Paige, are you awake?" Brenda's voice was a soft whisper as she peered round the door. "Declan's on the phone."

When her mother had left, assuming she was asleep, and all was quiet again, Paige found she was dry-eyed at last, but with a strange kind of guilty emptiness.

Why had he phoned? She curled up into a tight little ball under the covers as her stomach twisted in a giant knot. She only had herself to blame. She had let those few words that he had spoken six years ago colour her opinion of him until she had been blind to the real man. She had painted him black—and now there was a chasm between them which was quite uncrossable.

And she would have liked to get to know him. Even as she let her mind voice the thought, his words came back to her in painful clarity. "You're playing with fire..." He clearly didn't want to get to know her! And why should he? Apart from the insults she had thrown at him, the barely concealed dislike and aggressiveness, she just wasn't his type. His women were sophisticated, worldly-wise and totally free spirits. Could she ever be like that?

No, she couldn't, she admitted to herself honestly. But just at this moment, it was bleak comfort. He had gone without even saying goodbye, and that said it all.

"Paige?" Matthew's voice was gentle as he faced her over the small table for two. "Who is he?"

"What?" She stared back into the handsome boyish face in surprise.

"There's someone who's put those shadows under your eyes." Matthew touched her face lightly. "You love him, don't you? Is it Declan?"

"Please, don't be so ridiculous!" She took a big gulp of the dry white wine that had accompanied the trout. "Declan? We don't get on, Matthew, we never have."

Matthew's eyes roamed across her flushed face. "Well, I'm not one to argue, but I'd bet my last fiver that the look in his eyes that day at your parents' house was not dislike. And excuse me for saying so, but you seemed to be pretty aware of him too."

"Matthew, leave it, please. We've never hit it off, but there does seem to be some sort of physical attraction. It means less than nothing."

"OK, Paige, have it your own way." Matthew let the subject drop.

How she got through the rest of the evening she didn't know, but the second Matthew left her flat a few hours later, after a nightcap she had deliberately prolonged, she had to face the fact that her brain had been screaming at her ever since his concerned enquiry. She loved Declan.

She loved Declan? "No!" She paced the flat furiously, telling herself that Declan was the last man in the world to love. Totally self-sufficient, needing and wanting no one, and yet...

She got ready for bed slowly, lingering under the shower as she let the warm water mingle with the tears on her uplifted face. She had always loved Declan; it was time to face facts. The knowledge had been tucked away deep in her subconscious since that troubled summer when she was sixteen and he had hurt her so badly.

"You're Brenda's kid?" She still remembered their first exchange. "Don't look so scared, tich, this lot won't eat you."

"I'm not scared," she had lied bravely, and Declan had chuckled.

"You aren't? Good for you! Most of them scare the hell out of me."

She had asked his name then, and after introductions had been completed she had tagged along with him for the rest of the afternoon until that catastrophic return to the house when she had overheard his conversation with Gerald.

She lay in bed with her head spinning and her brain buzzing with a thousand words. After an hour of tossing and turning she flung the covers aside and reached for pen and paper. She would write to him. Casual, friendly, explaining that their last meeting had been a mistake she was sure he regretted as much as she and that, if only for their parents' sake, it would be better to see each other now and again in the future. Once the letter was written, addressed care of her mother, she felt better, and it wasn't until it had been posted the next morning that the misgivings blossomed. They lasted for a few days, but then routine blurred the edges and she threw herself frantically into her work.

It was as she was at home working on a particularly difficult sketch one evening two weeks later that the doorbell broke her concentration. Swearing softly under her breath, she marched to the door and swung it open with a ferocious scowl on her face.

''Hi, there.''

If the ground beneath her feet had opened, she couldn't have been more shocked as she stared into Declan's wary, unsmiling eyes.

"Is there any reason for the scary face or do you usually greet callers with such charm?" he asked mockingly.

"Declan!" She stared at him helplessly.

"Paige!" he answered softly. "Do we stand here all night saying each other's names, or am I permitted into the sanctuary?" he asked drily.

"Oh, I'm sorry." She stepped back. "Come in, please. It's just so unexpected..."

"Could I have a cup of coffee?" He obviously realised he wasn't going to get much sense out of her. "I've driven straight here and the meal on the plane seems like a year ago."

"Driven straight here?"

"With a quick stop at Hertfordshire," he said blandly. The letter? Her stomach turned over in anticipation.

"But you should have eaten before driving again."

He looked at her for a long moment and then said, "I thought you might not have eaten as it's still quite early. Have you?"

"No."

"Would you care to go out for a meal? I see you're working. I hope I haven't interrupted anything." The silver eyes stroked slowly over her hot face.

For a whole millisecond she considered being offhand, but then she smiled brilliantly. "I'd love to, absolutely love to," she said.

He blinked slightly at her enthusiasm as he took the coffee she offered. "I think we need to talk, Paige," he said softly after a long, tense pause.

As they drew up outside the hotel and an attentive doorman moved forward to open her door Paige glanced at Declan in open amazement. "Here? We're going to eat here?" It was one of the most exclusive hotels in London. "Have you booked a table?"

"No." He glanced at her. "But I know the manager. There will be a table."

"Good evening, Mr. Stone." The doorman smiled widely as Declan handed him the car keys. "Miss." He nodded to Paige. "Are you staying with us, sir?"

"Not this time, Bob," Declan replied easily. "But I couldn't think of a restaurant I like better, so..."

"Thank you, Mr. Stone. *Bon appetit.*" The small man was grinning from ear to ear as he climbed into Declan's silver car, handling the vehicle with an aplomb that spoke of familiarity.

"I take it you stay here when you're in London?" she asked quietly.

He nodded. "It's convenient. I gave up my flat years ago, preferring just one home in America. Makes life simpler."

"Yes, it would," she murmured drily as he drew her over towards the breathtakingly smart restaurant.

This, then, was his home from home! She felt a sad, wry pain catch at her heart-strings as the last clinging hope that she could ever mean anything more than a friend died a swift death. He lived on the same planet but in a different world! She smiled grimly to herself. And she had convinced herself she had written the letter in friendship! She felt such a savage anger with herself that she could have screamed. She was such a fool.

"You're doing it again." His voice was cool.

"Sorry?" She glanced up to find the grey eyes firmly fixed on her face.

"Giving the impression that you're in the company of the devil himself." He tilted her face upwards. "Try, just for this evening, to look as though you are enjoying my company?"

"I'm sorry, Declan, I didn't mean—"

"And no apologies," he said softly.

The courses came and went, but Paige wasn't conscious of what she ate at all. Her whole being was concentrated on the dark, cold face opposite. Declan was his usual imperturbable, cynical self, and she noticed he didn't eat much, as though he was under some strain. Her mother had confided that she thought he was under some pressure when she phoned a couple of days ago, and that Gerald was a little concerned. Perhaps he needed to talk to someone?

"Is everything all right, Declan?" she asked as they lingered over coffee.

"All right? Why do you ask?"

"I don't know," she floundered. "You just seem a little preoccupied, not your usual self."

"And what, in your opinion, is my 'usual self'?"

She stared at him silently, and neither of them said anything for a full minute. Then he leaned back in his chair. "To answer your question honestly, no, everything is not all right," he said expressionlessly, "and you are quite right, I am not my normal self. OK?"

"What's wrong?" she asked. "Business problems?"

"Not exactly." He looked at her tightly.

"Can I help at all?" she asked quietly. He looked at her for a long moment, and as she held his gaze she felt her heart begin to pound madly. There was an expression in his eyes that defied description. He was hurting badly, she could feel it, but he wasn't going to let her in, she could feel that too. Was it a woman?

"Love trouble?" She kept her voice light.

"Just so." The deep voice was laconic. "And you?" He paused but still she couldn't look into his face at that moment. "How's Matthew?"

"Matthew?" Just for a crazy moment she wondered who Matthew was. "Oh—I think he's fine, I haven't seen him in days." He's fallen for someone, her head was screaming.

"Why not?"

"Oh, I've been busy, he's been busy—you know how it is," she said faintly.

"Yes." He answered her in a strangely abstracted tone, then turned to the waiter who had appeared at his elbow. "That was excellent as always. Could you arrange for the car to be brought round?''

"Of course, Mr. Stone."

Paige toyed with the idea of inviting him in for a nightcap. She was torturing herself, she knew, and if he started to talk about this other woman... Her mind raced on. But she didn't know when she would see him again.

"Would you like to come in for a coffee, brandy or something?" she asked lightly as he brought the sleek silver car to a halt at the back of the flats.

"Thank you." His smile jolted her heart again and she lectured herself fiercely all the way to her front door.

"Here, let me." She was fumbling with her key, his presence making her all fingers and thumbs, and as he opened the door and they stepped into the tiny hall he put his hand on her arm, drawing her round to face him. "Paige?" The rough edge to his voice and the darkness in the silver-grey eyes brought her heart to her mouth. "Paige, you have to understand—"

The telephone's shrill ring made her jump and his grip loosened as a wry twist curved his mouth. "Saved by the bell."

"Did you need saving?" she asked uncertainly as his low growl of a laugh caught at her breath.

"Not me, honeypot, you."

"Hello?" As she spoke into the receiver she was aware of a slow trembling starting in the pit of her stomach as he moved to stand behind her, drawing her against him.

"Paige?" Matthew's voice was loud enough for Declan to hear. "It's Matt. How are you, sweetheart?" It was his usual form of address and meant nothing, but as Declan stiffened and moved away she knew he had misunderstood the affection in Matthew's voice.

"Fine, Matt." As Declan walked into the small lounge she took a long, deep breath. Hurry up, Matt, please, she thought weakly.

"I feel I've been too busy to keep an eye on my favorite girl," Matthew said lightly.

"Stop worrying," she said softly.

"What are friends for?" Matthew's voice was gentle. "Someone has got to keep an eye on you!"

"And you do it very well," she countered, "but now is not the time."

"Company?" Matthew asked warily. "Oh, no, Paige, don't tell me it's Declan?"

"Yes." She heard him groan. "I'll see you at work, OK?"

"OK." The phone went down quickly.

"You needn't have cut it short on my account," Declan said icily as she joined him in the tiny lounge. "I'm sure you two have lots to talk about, having missed a few days."

"Not really." She looked at him blankly.

"He's about your age, isn't he?" Declan continued. "You obviously have a lot in common—work, friends and so on."

"I suppose so." She was at a loss to understand the sudden change of mood. "Matt's a good friend."

"I'm sure he is," he said curtly as he glanced at the gold watch on his wrist. "It's later than I thought, Paige, I'd better take a raincheck on that coffee."

"Oh, but—"

"Goodbye." He barely glanced at her as he left the flat, his body tight and rigid and his profile enigmatic as he passed her.

When are you going to get it through your thick head that you mean nothing to him? she asked herself bitterly. She was a vague member of his family through necessity, that was all, and now there was someone else in his life.

As the tears came, hot and fierce, she wished with all her heart that she could hate him, but it was too late. Far, far too late. The saddest, loneliest words in any language.

Five

The next few days crawled by, and Paige had never been more thankful that she had a job which demanded total concentration. It didn't ease the ache that had her heart in an iron grip, but there were times when it was dulled enough for her to function normally.

When the telephone rang at five one morning a week after she had last seen Declan, she groaned softly as she reached out for the receiver. Yesterday had been a bad day: his face had materialised on the paper every time she had settled down to work and it had been one in the morning before she was satisfied with the designs she had struggled with all day.

"Paige?" The voice on the other end of the line was unmistakably Declan's and she sat bolt upright in bed.

"Declan?" She took a deep breath. "How ... how are you?" she stammered. What was the time difference with America? Why was he ringing? He cut off her racing thoughts abruptly.

"I'm fine." He didn't sound fine. Had his new love ended it? She felt a moment's fierce longing that she had and then felt bitterly ashamed. It wouldn't make any difference anyway, so why hope? "I've got some news I thought you might like to hear."

He was getting married! She had heard the expression of blood running cold, but it was the first time in her life that she had actually experienced it. It wasn't pain she had read in his voice, but excitement. "Yes?" Even to herself her voice sounded dead.

"Are you alone?" The sudden note of uncertainty in his voice didn't register until after she had replied.

"Of course I'm alone, it's five in the morning."

"Yes, of course. You just sound a little strange."

"You woke me up with a jolt," she said quietly. Get on with it, Declan, she thought numbly.

"It's my job," he said grimly. "Good news."

"Your job? Promotion?"

"And how. I thought you might like to know, after the letter?"

"The letter?" What on earth was he on about? she thought helplessly. Why mention the letter now?

"The letter you wrote to me. Brenda forwarded it to my hotel from Hertfordshire. I've just read it."

"You've just read it." He'd only just received the letter, then?

There was silence for a few seconds and then his voice was infinitely weary. "It doesn't matter. I just thought—" He stopped abruptly. "The job means very little travel for a few years, so you'll have some peace. This dislike, antagonism, call it what you will—you'll be free of its burden. You won't have to pretend for our parents' sake after all."

"Declan?" She hesitated, frightened of saying the wrong thing. All her instincts told her he was probing, but the past as well as the present held her in its grip. He had crucified her at sixteen and continued to hurt her ever since, and now that there was someone else—how could she bare her soul to this man? If he even suspected her true feelings for him she would die. Her pride was the only thing she had left.

"Why, Paige?" Now his voice wasn't cool or reserved but raw with pain. "I've got to know. Why do you hate me so?"

"I don't hate you, Declan." She heard herself say the words with a strange feeling of calm and knew she was going on to explain. She suddenly realised that there was nothing to lose any more; her pride was unimportant beside the hurt in his voice. She had to set things straight, explain, and then maybe at least he would understand what had motivated her in the past. Anything was better than this giant tangle.

"I don't hate you," she repeated slowly, "although I thought I did once. But you hurt me, you see, and it was some sort of defence mechanism, I think, although I've only realised that recently. You remember the first time we met at your father's home? When he held the barbecue to introduce my mother to his friends?" As she continued to explain the ripples that one conversation had made in their lives, there was a deathly silence on the other end of the line. As she brought the story up to the present she found she couldn't tell him of her love for him. If he had made some comment, it might have been easier, but his silence fed the growing suspicion that she was making a ghastly mistake.

"Declan?" As her voice halted the silence lengthened, and as she heard the receiver replaced at the other end her stomach jolted. She had bared her soul, almost, and for what?

"Declan!" She sat rocking aimlessly on the bed, the pain too deep for tears, and after a long time rose slowly like an old woman and walked through into the kitchen to make a cup of coffee.

The ring at the doorbell didn't surprise her; she felt as though she had fallen into a kind of vacuum where nothing would ever move her again, and she didn't even wonder who was calling at six a.m. as she padded into the hall and opened the front door.

"Paige?"

Slamming the door in Declan's face was instinctive but he reacted just as quickly, stopping it with his foot as he moved forward. "You're in America," she whispered. "You phoned me from America. You said the letter had been sent—"

"Paige?" He reached out and shook her gently. "What on earth is the matter? Did I frighten you? It's me, I'm not in America. I said the letter had been sent to my hotel, here in England, in London."

"Did you?" She took a deep breath as she tried to pull herself together. "But it's so early. I thought—"

"If I hadn't phoned then I'd have lost my nerve." He ran a hand distractedly across his face, and she noticed he was very white. "I've just got in from Heathrow and thought I'd open my post before I had a shower." The silver eyes were more intense than she had ever seen them. "I needed to talk to you, damn it, don't you understand?" He shook his head at her blank expression. "But no, of course not, why should you? You really don't have any idea how I feel, do you?"

"How you feel?" She looked down at her bare feet, letting her cloud of red silky hair hide her face from his. "I think I know how you feel, Declan," she said wearily.

"I doubt it." The deep voice was husky. "But I want you to do one last thing for me and listen while I talk to you, try to make you understand about the past, everything. And then I'll get out of your life, for good. Is that a deal?'' His voice cracked painfully.

She looked up then, her face as white as his. ''You'd better come and sit down.'' He followed her into the lounge after shutting the door but paced the small floor as he began to talk, his voice low and even.

''I know this will make no difference to how you feel about me, Paige, but I must explain.'' She curled her feet under her as she huddled in the soft armchair.

''That night at the barbecue, when you heard me talking to my father—'' He stopped abruptly, his face ashen. ''Hell, Paige!'' He stopped his pacing to face her. ''You must believe I didn't mean a word I said, even then. I was angry and hurt and I just lashed out blindly. I didn't mean the things I said about your mother or yourself. In fact I'd thought how sweet and shy you were, so different from most of the crowd there. If I'd have known you heard me...'' He drove one hand into the other in a clenched fist and then resumed the pacing.

''I hated myself afterwards for what I said that night. Can you believe that?'' He paused and faced her and she nodded slowly.

"Yes, I believe you."

"But Father and I had never got on, and within weeks he had given me an ultimatum. Accept Brenda completely or get out of his life. I chose the latter." He shook his head at the memory. "Crazy really, and so like both of us. I'm more like him than I care to admit. But I was filled with a strange kind of hate-love for him. Hate at the way I felt he'd let my mother down, and love for him as my father. But I couldn't have even put it into words then, it was buried too deep. But you made me realise that I had spent a good deal of my adult life running away, from normal life, commitment, love... And all along I'd got it wrong. Misjudged things totally."

He knelt down in front of her chair and her stomach muscles clenched at his closeness, at the familiar smell of his aftershave and the gleaming darkness of his hair as his head came down on a level with hers. "I've been a blind fool, Paige, and all the time I thought I'd got it together, that I was where I wanted to be."

"You did?" She knew she should be saying more, but the shock of seeing him like this had robbed her of all thought.

He nodded slowly. "I've wasted years chasing success and living the life of a nomad, terrified of putting any roots down, of establishing ties. I chose my women for their sophistication in the game of love, for their ability to be as cool as I was. None of them touched my heart, Paige. Not until—" He looked at her tightly.

This was it, she thought painfully. This was the moment of truth about the other woman. She sprang up so suddenly that he almost stumbled before he straightened.

"I'm glad you came to clear the air, Declan," she said frantically fast, her face distraught as she walked to the door.

He stood very still for a long moment, his face grey and strained and his eyes brilliantly silver, and then as she turned to face him covered the ground between them in two steps. As he took her into his arms she was too amazed to react, but then, as she felt the fierceness of his lips, her mind stood still. It was a long, deep kiss and her head was swimming when he raised his head, his face impassioned and bitterly sad.

"One last thing to forgive me for." He stepped back a pace as she swayed in front of him. "But it's got to last me a long, long time. There'll never be anyone but you, Paige, but you don't want to hear this." He shook his head in violent disgust at himself. "You've made it clear how you feel about me, and I of all people know that physical attraction doesn't last too long. Maybe you don't even feel that any more."

She stared at him, her eyes huge.

"You'll never know how you affected me that night I opened the door and saw the girl of my dreams standing there," he said huskily. "And then I got to know you and the hell of it was, the dream was real. I'd never imagined that someone like you still existed in this crazy world. But I knew all along there was no chance. Even if you hadn't loathed me on sight, you deserve someone like Matthew, who hasn't been contaminated by life the way I have. And I love you enough to stay out of your life. I promise you that."

He had left the flat and reached the lift doors before her stunned senses made sense of it all, and as she called his name they closed, so that she wondered for a second if she had just dreamt the last few minutes.

"Declan?" As she spoke his name she realised he had done it again—left her before she could speak to him, tell him how she felt. "Declan!" She was pounding her fists on the closed doors when a dry cough brought her back to herself.

"Is there anything wrong, Miss Green?" She didn't even bother to reply to her next-door neighbour's disapproving enquiry, flying back into her flat and slamming the door.

Was he at the hotel he had taken her to? He had to be! He *had* to be. She couldn't have explained how she felt as she dressed in frantic frustration at her own slowness, her heart thudding and her head spinning and the tears running down her face in a flood that was quite unstoppable. He loved her. *He loved her*!

"Can I help you?" The receptionist looked incredibly fresh and smart for so early in the morning and Paige felt even more like a fish out of water as she looked into the cool, smiling face, eyebrows carefully raised in polite enquiry.

"I'm here to see Mr. Stone, Declan Stone," she said with all the assurance she could muster. "I was here with him a few weeks ago. I'm his stepsister." She didn't know what made her add that last sentence, but as she did so, the girl's smile relaxed into a genuine welcome.

"Of course." She beamed. "Is he expecting you?"

"Not exactly." Paige kept her voice firm and confident. "I was rather hoping to surprise him, actually."

"Oh." The smile faltered a little. "Well, I really ought to ring through to his suite, Miss...?"

"Green, Paige Green," Paige answered automatically. "Do you have to? I promise it will be all right."

"Well, if you're sure..." The girl's eyes ran over Paige's thick warm jumper, sensible trousers and flat shoes and seemed reassured. She obviously wasn't the type wicked women were made of, Paige reflected. "He's in his normal suite," the cool voice continued, "third floor."

"Thank you." Paige smiled with all the calm she could muster and made for the lifts, wondering what she would do on the third floor if there were several different doors.

"Third floor, miss." The liftboy smiled at her.

"Thank you." She hesitated. "Which are Mr. Stone's rooms?"

"End of the corridor, miss."

There was no answer to her knock and the sense of anticlimax was painfully frustrating. She tried again, harder and longer this time, and then the door swung open and there he was. He'd obviously just stepped out of the shower, a light towelling robe ending just above his knees and his hair dripping wet.

"Declan!" As she flung herself into his arms they opened instinctively to receive her, but after the first heart-stopping moment, she felt a shudder run through his muscled body as he carefully pushed her to arm's length.

"You shouldn't have come, Paige, there's nothing more to be said." The mask was very firmly in place, she noted, as she took in the veiled cold eyes, straight mouth and hard, tight face, but for once the guise didn't intimidate her. She had seen the real Declan a short while ago and she was going to reach him regardless of the old barriers so firmly in place.

"I disagree," she said quietly. "In fact I seem to remember it was you who did all the talking. I never got a word in edgeways."

"Paige, I think you'd better leave." As she turned to face him the façade hadn't faltered. "If you've come to offer words of sympathy I can do without them."

"Words of sympathy?" She stared at him. "You are the last person in the world I would ever pity, Declan."

"What, then?" She saw the flash of uncertainty in his eyes. "Your pound of flesh, is that it?"

"You could put it like that." She moved forward to his side. "But I want all your flesh, Declan, not just a pound." She smiled her love into his eyes.

She saw the disbelief in his face along with something that made her want to cry as she went up on tiptoe to kiss his mouth, and then his hands had come out to hold her to him in a bearhug that left her unable to breathe. "Paige? Paige, is this real? You aren't playing with me?"

"I love you," she said into the warmth of his throat before raining tiny frantic kisses on his face. "I always have. I loved you the minute I set eyes on you at sixteen and I've been trying to fight it ever since."

"Don't fight it." His voice was husky as his arms tightened still more round her slim shape, lifting her off her feet. "Don't ever fight it, my love. Loving you the way I do has turned my world upside-down and nearly killed me, and if you wanted revenge you've had it a million times since that night at the birthday party. I've nearly gone mad night after night, imagining you in

Matthew's arms or, worse still, someone I didn't know about. I've been living in hell with no hope of release ... Oh, Paige ..."

Long, satisfying minutes later he raised his head to look down into her glowing face, his eyes dark with passion. "Marry me? Soon?"

"How soon?" she breathed shakily.

"Special licence soon?"

She nodded happily. "Nearly soon enough. But in the meantime ..."